My Best Friend

Hot Erotic Short Stories Illustrated with

Hentai Pictures

_____

Emily White

Printing and distribution: Heinz-Beusen-Stieg 5 22926 Ahrensburg, Germany

TABLE OF CONTENTS

INTRODUCTION

Welcome to a captivating journey where my enthralling stories seamlessly intertwine with enchanting illustrations that redefine the very essence of desire in the world of hentai erotica.

Within the secret pages of these forbidden tales, I invite you to immerse yourself in a fiery universe of unrestrained passion. Every word is a whispered moan, and each illustration is a visual embrace that transforms the realms of fantasy into tangible reality.

This collection is not for the faint of heart. It's a bold manifesto, an invitation urging you to delve into the dark depths of lust, where pleasure is painted with audacious strokes and details that promise to quicken the rhythm of your heart. The illustrations are provocative gateways, guiding you into sensual dimensions where every hidden desire finds its expression without remorse.

Are you ready to plunge into a whirlwind of seduction and temptation, where the pages themselves transform into a stage for your most secret fantasies? Allow yourself to be carried away into a realm where sin transforms into art, and art seamlessly merges harmoniously with the ecstasy of desire.

Lift the cover and prepare for an experience ignited by the flame of passion. This is not just another collection; it's your exclusive ticket to the boldest manifestations of anime eros, written masterfully by me, **Emily White**.

WHEN SHE RUNS AWAY

Like every summer, I had moved to the countryside to my maternal grandparents that year.

Small village of about a thousand souls and houses scattered throughout the countryside.

I had a group of friends, the usual ones I knew as a child, some lived there all year round, others like me only in the summer.

There were very few recreational opportunities, we kids would meet at the park bar.

Between girls the usual chatter looking for something new to invent or some passing boy to meet, but generally the faces were always the same.

Around the age of thirteen-fourteen it had also been fun to have the first summer flings with those kids but by then I wasn't interested in them anymore.

Maybe it was because I was growing up but that summer seemed more boring than usual and nothing could lift it.

One evening, after going to the bar, I went back home on foot, my grandparents' house was about five kilometers away, the road had no sidewalk but was paved and bordered a whole series of houses.

It must have been 20 o'clock in early July in the middle of the day.

I had been walking for about fifteen minutes when I felt an urgent need to pee.

I had drank too much Coca-Cola and also a half beer offered by a guy and surely for the hurry I had left the house without making it.

Ten more minutes on the road and just bursting, start looking around.

There was no question of doing it in the street, as too many cars were passing by and there were no secluded corners.

Fences, hedges, walls, all enclosed, at one point I passed a long masonry fence about two meters high, beyond you could see the tops of the trees.

On either side of the gate the fence lowered forming two concave curves so the height was reduced.

I peeked in and in the orchard I saw a woman hoeing.

The gate was pulled over I pushed it and entered to get the woman's attention.

She put down her hoe and approached, she could be about seventy years old and in spite of her clothing you could see that she was a beautiful woman.

"Excuse me," I said when I was close enough, "I have to pee."

"don't worry" she replied, amused, "there's room and I'm alone here, put yourself wherever you want but move away from the gate".

I took a few steps to settle where the wall was higher, with my back to her I pulled down my jeans and briefs, squatted on the floor, and began to pee.

When I finished I didn't have any tissues, I shook a little the pussy to get the last drops down, I stood up I lifted everything and I turned around.

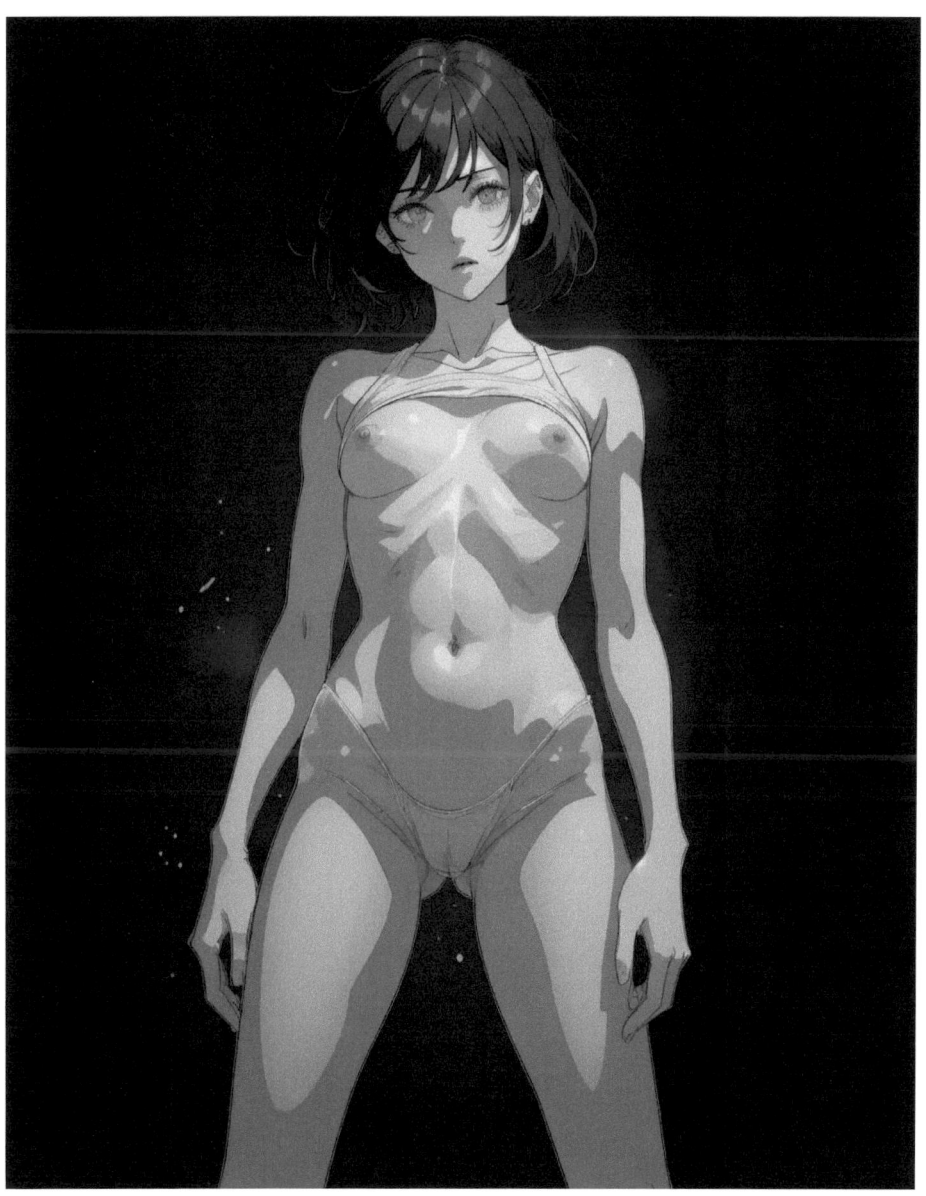

The woman had stayed behind me, I thanked her and almost ran away.

On the way home, without knowing why, I start to feel excited.

When I got home, I went to the bathroom to wash myself, my pussy was all wet, with my legs wide open on the bidet: I couldn't resist and, while I was washing myself, I fingered myself and came immediately.

At night in bed, I thought back to what had happened, as I slowly touched myself I realized that I would like to repeat that.

The next day I found myself walking past that house; it seemed crazy but I couldn't resist.

There was more than a chance she would kick me out in a bad way, it was certainly not a public restroom, but my instincts suggested to try it.

In addition, to be ready, I had drunk almost two liters of water and now I just had to run.

I arrived in front of the gate and called her attention.

Se beckoned me to come in.

She waved her hand, as if to say sit down and settle in wherever you want.

I had put on a fairly short skirt, I settled to the side because I had decided to peek while I was doing it.

I rolled my skirt up to my waist, lowered my panties to my knees, and squatted down holding them pulled forward by the elastic.

I had a quart to make, I looked at it quickly a couple of times.

What excitement she had watching me pee.

Her look was certainly not malicious, but it still had an effect on me.

I got up and settled down more calmly than the day before, thanked her and said goodbye.

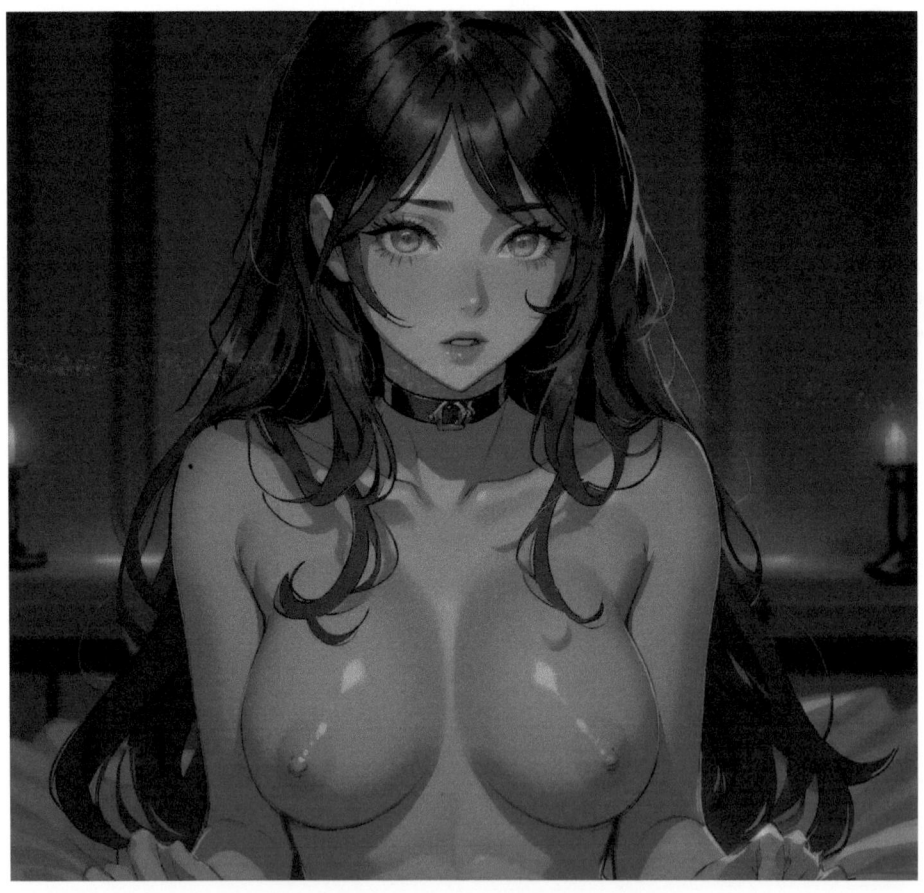

At night I had two fingerings and a bunch of projects.

The next night I was there again but she wasn't and I really risked pissing my pants.

For a couple of days I didn't see her, I would then cycle by first to check on her but on the third day there she was again in the orchard.

I came home sent down a bottle of water and got ready.

I made my way slowly to fully savor that moment, showing myself through the gate.

She nodded to come in, until then I had stopped about ten meters from her but that day she was working where I usually did.

I settled into the usual corner, rolled my skirt around my waist and slipped off my briefs.

I ducked down in front a few feet from her.

I didn't want to do it right away, I looked up and watched me quietly waiting for me to finish.

Start to do it only it was embarrassing because I escaped a long jet.

Without waiting for me to finish, she said "you had to do it eh ".

I said "yes, I had to" and we continued talking while I finished to free myself.

At night while I was touching myself as usual I decided to take another step.

After a few days I saw her again I got ready as usual, I nodded and entered.

She was pretty far away but I approached.

Arrived at her house, I slipped off the skirt and panties and put them on a stone. She said nothing, I turned my back and peed, I knew I had a nice butt and I wanted her to see it.

Then I got up and stayed and talked to her about ten minutes naked from the waist down.

She behaved as usual with naturalness and I, who understood that the thing had gone beyond normal, did not know what to think.

Sure that, by now, she could not tell me anything, the next day I came back I did everything like the day before.

After peeing, she slowly began to caress my belly then my pubes and, finally, since she did not say anything, I began to touch the button.

I had never been so wet, a lake, the drops ran down to my thighs,

The woman was talking about one of her cats while I touched myself.

After a few minutes I almost came in front of her; the woman instead courteously greeted me, "come back" then gave me a kiss on the cheek.

Another couple of days passed, as usual I had hydrated profusely, I
arrived and went straight into the garden.

I didn't see her right away but, since the gate was half open, I thought she must be there, I walked a certain section of the driveway.

I realized it too late: when I saw her I realized she wasn't alone.

Next to her was a short, stooped grandmother at least ninety years old; the two women were talking.

She motioned me closer, introduced me as the granddaughter of ...; how embarrassed I realized he knew my grandmother.

They started asking me questions, the usual ones, where I lived, the school, if I liked the place. The granny had a lively look and was very lucid.

I had to run away.

I was clutching my legs to hold her back, to go away and do it before leaving was out of the question; we had moved to the avenue and from there you could see everything up to the gate.

It was the lady who got me out of the way, "that's how we met, the girl has a bladder disorder and the doctor ordered her to do it often, so on her way home she stopped at my place".

" but then maybe she has an urgency and we are holding her back," said the granny.

"yes sorry dear, go ahead freely this is a dear friend".

Obviously I was very excited about it, although I really had to do it I decided to stretch it out.

I joked a little then I moved a few steps away from them near a tree, slipping my hands under the skirt along the sides I slipped off the panties, then rolled the skirt around my waist showing my butt, then I turned in front of them and crouched down with my thighs wide open.

I had shaved my pubes, and my pussy was completely exposed; with my fingers I parted the small lips, then I began to urinate.

With extreme naturalness the two women looked at me, I kept the skin on my pubis pulled upwards so that the jet went forward.

Every now and then however I made sure to shift the direction by wetting my thighs.

I stopped then resumed.

The grandmother said: "wow, you were bursting".

The gushes lasted quite a while. When they ended, I was so tired that I was still bent over with my inner thighs dripping.

"So you can't leave" said the lady, "wait here" and headed home.

I was left alone with the granny, I had gotten back on my feet, "in our day we didn't use that" and she looked at my pubes, "but now I know you girls all shave down there".

Then she added "can I touch it?".

I was speechless, "yes" was all I could say.

The grandmother sat on a trunk and made me come closer, then she put her hand on my pubis.

I felt a hand on a buttock then on my inner thighs.

She touched me heedless of the fact that I was all wet with pee, then stroked my sex.

She quickly found my clitoris and began to titillate it with a finger all around.

When the lady returned she found us like that, but she didn't say anything instead she let her elderly friend continue to fiddle with my sex.

"How nice is to be young" the old woman said.

She continued to tease me until I came standing in front of them.

Afterwards, I was obviously mortified, but they washed, dried and fixed me with a thousand attentions and cares.

I went back many more times to that house... each time piss and finger... what a nostalgia.

MY SEXY PHOTO

ELDA AND ALDA

Elda, my son's ex-girlfriend, spends more time in my house than in hers, I often come home after ambulance shifts to find breakfast or lunch or even dinner ready, which is no small feat after eight grueling hours of work.

Elda has the keys and since her workplace is much closer to my house than hers, when it gets dark, she slips into my bed.

We go shopping together and since I spend every free moment in the country house, she often comes to visit me.

So, as not to have too much to tidy up, we occupy the same bed in the room upstairs, where there are no toilets.

We use the chamber pot and laugh when we go down the stairs in the morning, each holding our own pot.

The confidence between the two of us is very high to the point that, one afternoon, in the rural house, when I told her about the two men with whom I vent my sexual desires, she wanted to know the intimate details: if when I give blowjobs, I allow them to cum in my mouth and if I don't disdain to give my ass as well.

In response to my affirmative answer, when I had specified that in sex between consenting adults, everything is feasible, she confided to me that she had never experienced a true orgasm while fucking, that with my son.

They had experienced everything and more, and that the reason why they had decided not to share their entire lives, was that he had discovered her masturbating, immediately after they had had unbridled sex.

She then added that it happens to her from time to time, even if not cyclically, that she is assailed by the inescapable desire to enjoy herself and how she is forced to do it in order not to cum.

She told me that when it had happened to her on the bus, she had put on her sunglasses, had put a cleenex on her nose to hide her moans and distraught expression and then, spasmodically tightening her thighs, she had had a devastating orgasm.

She had gone downstairs like a madwoman, storming into a bar, she had locked herself in the toilet, where she had continued to masturbate until the barman had gone to knock on the door, to make sure she was okay.

He had put 5 euros in her hand, she had holed up in a cab where she had procured other orgasms, covering her face with a book that she always carried with her, together with her glasses and tissues.

She had finally concluded the tormentingly erotic day, fingering herself at home, immersed in the bathtub, then continuing in bed, until sleep had put an end to the exhausting erotic marathon.

I had asked her which fantasies she resorted to, when she was assailed by those uncontrollable cravings.

She had replied that she didn't think about anything, she concentrated on the approach of pleasure and that it was her organism that provided for her to have orgasms: she furiously rubbed her clitoris, in order to shorten the time between one enjoyment and the other.

She confided to me that one afternoon she had had 31 of them, losing then the count, for the rapidity with which they followed each other.

I had told her that I thought it was a wonderful thing, Elda had laughed and added, "Wonderful and embarrassing!".

"One afternoon in June, while I was studying in the library, I had five consecutive orgasms, to the point that the exaggerated flow of vaginal juices had formed a wet spot on the front of my leggings; I escaped by covering the spot with a book, ashamed of the penetrating odor I was spreading around me."

"On the way home, I had fingered myself twice in the toilets of a supermarket, again in the hallway of a main door and the last one inside an abandoned car in an alley, where prostitutes, in the dark, brought their clients.

So be careful Alda, if you are around when I get the urge, I'll jump on you and rape you". As a joke, I told her, "I'd run away, but not so fast that you wouldn't catch up with me."

We'd laughed, then I'd taken refuge in the bathroom to masturbate, not fantasizing about having sex with her because, aside from the kisses I'd exchanged with a friend from school when I was 15, which had served to keep me from looking like a dork, in the vicinity of my first date with a boy, I'd never considered Sapphic sex.

I had, however, been turned on by seeing with my mind's eye, Elda enjoying herself, overwhelmed by the repeated waves of pleasure.

When I had left, she had taken my hand, brought her fingers to her nose, sniffed and kissed them, looked at me jauntily, then we had both burst out laughing.

That same night, awakened by the approach of a thunderstorm, I perceived an unusual noise and in the screened light of the bedside lamp, Elda appeared to me in an exasperatingly erotic attitude.

With one hand she was holding the enameled metal vat, splashing jets of urine into it that made that peculiar sound, and with the other she had brought a breast to her mouth, licking the nipple, looking at me at the same time with the ravenous look of a she-wolf in heat.

I let out a choked moan, but I didn't take my eyes off her who, using the hand with which she had held her tit, was repeatedly passing her fingers along the cut of her cunt and sucking them lasciviously; I imagined tasting the taste of her piss and then the fire set my body on fire.

The orgasm began to flow down my spine and the moment it exploded in my clitoris, I propped up my heels and the back of my neck, arched my back, screamed as I enjoyed inhumanly, then gasped and gasped as Elda told me:

"Now you know how I feel when these feelings assault me."

She put down the vase and lay down, far away from me, turning her back on me and leaving me with a crazy desire for her, with the desire to play with her large breasts and the longing to sink my tongue between the lips of her cunt, hoping to taste the stimulating effluvia.

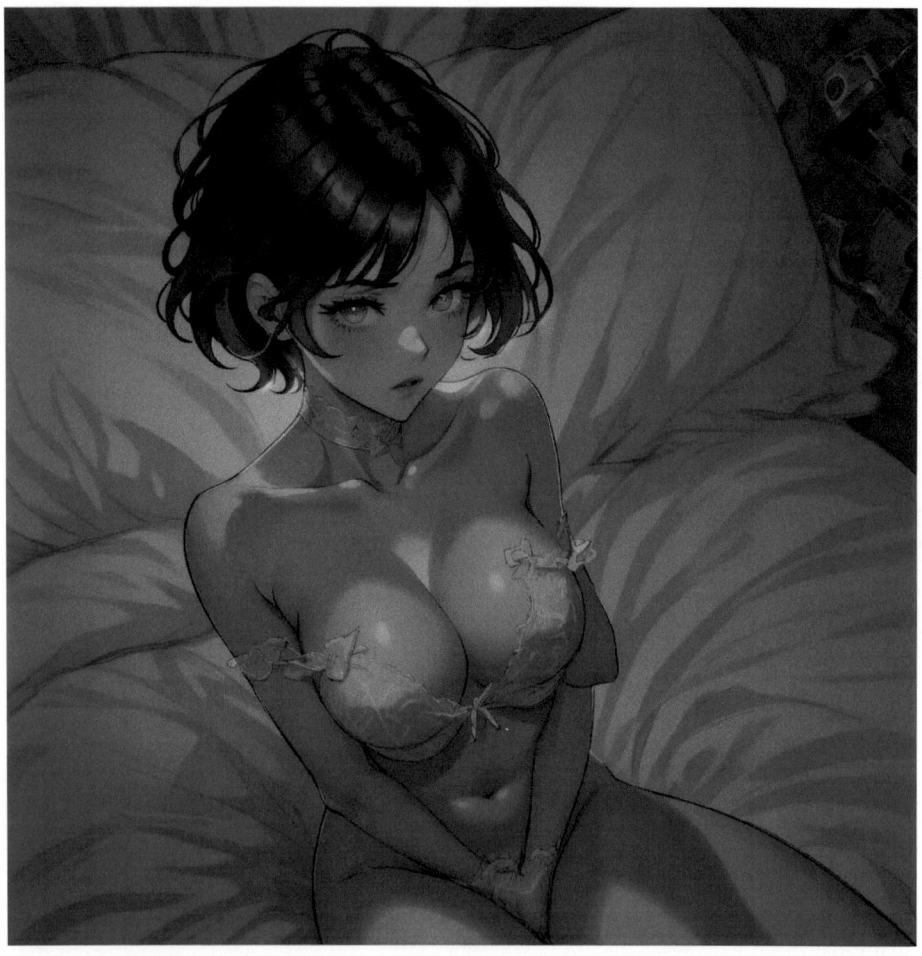

Now I knew for sure what would be in the future, the erotic fantasies to which I would have resorted, both in self-eroticism, and when fucking with my partners, I would have realized that the orgasm was struggling to come.

Lightning, thunder, water in profusion, I got out of bed and went to close the window, I came back, and at the flash of lightning, I realized that Elda was terrified.

In fact, as soon as I went to bed, she clung to my body and slid down hiding under the covers, clawing with one hand a breast and with the other a thigh, every time the thunder rumbled that preceded the furious pop of lightning.

I tried to soothe her, but selfishly I was focused on the softness and warmth of her tits rubbing my belly, and her groping my nakedness, instead of giving me pain, turned me on even more.

The noises receded, she eased the furious manipulation of my body, her hand on my breasts became light and caressing, the other moved to the crotch of my thighs, all the while her lips kissed my belly, lapping at my navel with her tongue as she played with the thick hairs of my sex.

I sensed the approach of an extraordinary experience and I was ready and with all my senses on the alert, when her middle finger touched the orifice between my buttocks testing the elasticity.

Then, she pushed it deep into the slimy niche already prepared for penetration, meanwhile the fingertip of his thumb took care of the clitoris, rubbing it between the same and the index finger, driving me crazy to the point that my temples were throbbing.

She masturbated me for a long time, adapting the rhythm to the intensification of my moans, until the moment when, she kicked the sheets and got down on her knees at my side.

Her fingers inside my pussy were two that became three, then four, she pushed her hand slit inside me, giving me the feeling of disemboweling me, then she lowered himself and while her hand fucked me more and more frantically.

Her mouth took care of my clitoris, licking, biting, sucking it, while I was afraid of falling into a swoon, unable to resist the delicious torment exasperated and intense.

It was at that point that one of her legs went over my head, her body adhered to mine, and she offered me her shaved cunt to lapped:

"Make the same movements as me!" She mumbled and I imitated her tongue whipping my clit, which stiffened by forcing the meatus of my urethra causing me to urinate, while I did the same to her.

"Piss slut!" She screamed inside the cave that had become my cunt and while a stream of piss dripped into my mouth, I felt two fingers violate my ass in depth.

I did the same and loosened my bladder. The orgasms followed each other relentlessly; I had never enjoyed in such a way and with such exaggerated intensity.

We slept in each other's arms and the next morning, as with chamber pots in hand, we descended the staircase naked, I told her: "Tonight you called me a slut."

She replied: "You think that out of respect for my age, I used a euphemism."

Elda sat down at the kitchen table, I asked her:

"What do you want for breakfast?"

She replied:

"Come here and sit on the table in front of me." I obeyed I sat in lace at the table, lodged my thighs on her shoulders and Elda, for breakfast ate my unwashed pussy, so still thick with the copious fluids of the many nightly orgasms.

When we reversed positions, since I had drained all the lifeblood, I made a long and hearty breakfast, devouring with insatiable voracity, the cunt and ass.

SEXY PHOTO OF ELDA

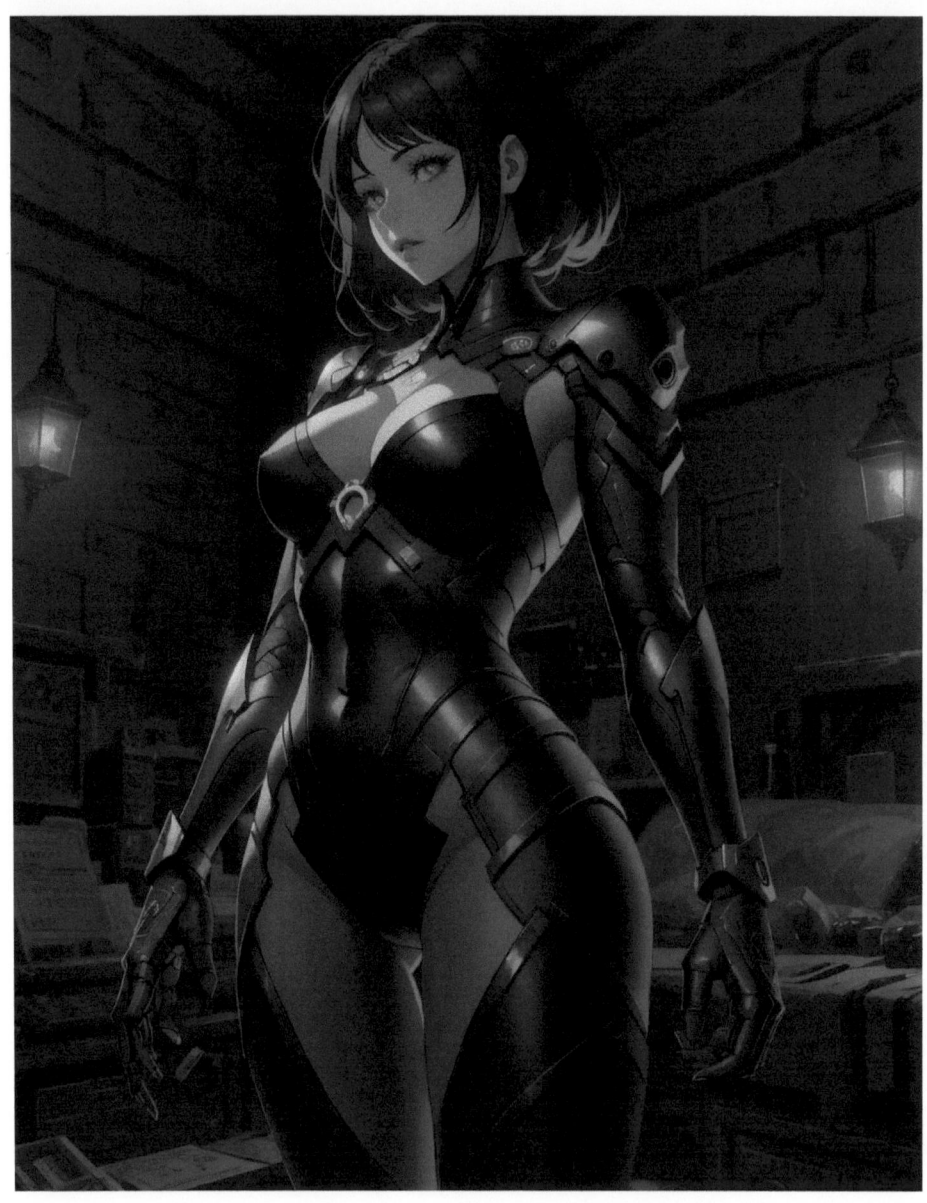

SEXY PHOTO OF ALDA

MY BEST FRIEND

"You start playing at a young age and never finish" this is what I always thought.

So I always bought myself a lot of games. Today I continue to buy...

I don't buy dolls or Barbie houses. I do my shopping at the sex shop now.

I talk about this a lot with my friends.

I have one in particular that doesn't want to hear about vibrators.

At the mere thought she clams up. Let's say she is a special friend, many times we found each other in bed... and got to know each other thoroughly.

Her name is Anna.... I'll tell you about our first time.

* * * * *

It was any other day, she calls me and invites me to her house, she says " Hi Sara, today I feel a little warm, I'm not well. Would you mind coming and keeping me company for a few minutes?"

Anna is a fifty year old lady, brunette, slender, polite and cultured. We have been good friends for a long time, and you never turn down a friend's request for help.

I dress sporty. I wear a pair of leggings and a tight top, tennis shoes.

I take the usual handbag ... in which I always put a small "toy".

I go to her. I ring the doorbell. She opens the door and surprisingly she is fully dressed: she is wearing a short ball skirt, high shoes and a transparent blouse. Through the blouse I see her excited breasts, her nipples are turgid. She is red in the face.

I am surprised and embarrassed. I tell her, "weren't you sick?"

And she" No I'm just hot!!!"

He grabs my hand, pulling me in. He throws me down on the couch and slips between my legs.

He pulls off my leggings and starts licking.

"Yes, Anna Yees."

I reach into my purse, open it and grab my vibrator.

I hand it to her, I want her to use it. I want her to stimulate my clit as she penetrates me with her fingers.... I'm enjoying it like crazy.

She surprises me again... "No! I don't touch that thing!" Blurts Anna and backs away from me and the vibrator.

I calm her down and approach her. She is standing in front of me.
I slip under her soft skirt, slip off her panties and begin to return her
service.

I push her onto the couch.

"More Sara!!!!" She continues to scream and beg for more with each of her orgasms.

She's really hot. She cum like a fountain. She's a really voluptuous woman.

She has already enjoyed three times. I take the vibrator and move it closer to her flower....

She recoils upon hearing this and becomes defensive again.

"No Sara, I just can't, I don't like it" Now it's over, she offers me something to drink.

Then she tells me, "I'm better now, thanks Sara."

Since that time we've had many more encounters. But I never brought my vibrator again.

* * * * *

Yesterday she calls me on the phone and says, "I need to introduce you to my best friend. Will I see you tomorrow at the bakery??"

"Who is this about? You never told me about having a best friend," I tell her.

Anna acts mysterious and says "I don't want to tell you anything, you don't know everything about me!"

"Alright, let's meet tomorrow. What time???" I ask her.

"Make it 9:00."

So today I went to meet his best friend.

I walk into the bakery.

I see her sitting at the small table a little way off in the corner of the room. She is far away from me.

She is very elegant. She is wearing a soft skirt and a nice top.

From the doorway she opens her legs slightly and shows me that she is not wearing briefs.

What's he up to this time?

I walk over and she's cheering me on as usual. "How are you doing dear? You always look elegant and beautiful!"

I for one can't wait to see what she has in mind.

"Where is this friend of yours?? We are here alone!"

"But you know, let's order something... then...." "Anna stalls.

We order a cappuccino and some pastries.

We eat and chat about this and that. We just look like two normal friends.

After finishing breakfast she says to me. "Accompany me to the restroom."

In this bakery, the restroom is really big, clean and beautiful.

We always use it and always go together.

But this time Anna surprises me.

We enter through the door. She leans against the door with her back, holding it shut.

She calls me and pulls me close to her. What's going on?

She whispers in my ear: "Meet my best friend" I don't understand. Then she takes my hand and guides it inside her legs.

She has me stick a finger into her vagina and to my surprise I find a vibrating egg.

She takes the remote control of the vibrator from a pocket, hands it to me and says, "Let me enjoy Sara, now, here."

My excitement is through the roof.

I pick her up, sit her on the marble countertop of the sink, and start pleasuring her.

I turn the vibrator on full blast. She moans and enjoys it. Now with the vibrator she has a lot of "confidence". She praises and continues to come. I lick her clit and with my fingers I make the egg move. "Yes Sara, more!!!" She keeps whispering.

We try not to be heard in the bakery....

Anna enjoys and enjoys again. We hear some noise, someone is entering the bathroom.

We quickly compose ourselves. "It's fine" It's the waitress.

"We were hearing strange noises, are you okay?"

"Great thanks!"

Anna still has the vibrator on in her vagina.

We paid and went to his house to finish.

We played them, played them again. Enjoyed and enjoyed them again.

Anna confessed to me that after my attempt to use a vibrator a few months ago, she got herself a "toy" that slowly, slowly made its way into her friendships.

She now has a close relationship with him, he is now her best friend!!!